Praise for *Arafat Mountain*

"These pages are a delicatessen, a thousand lives distilled into something quaint and beautiful. There's cosmic magic at play on every page, speedboats and celestial catastrophe all surround the monolith of Arafat Mountain. Every subtlety is sumptuous, every page a journey. These pages are full of death and I wonder—has death ever been so delightful?"
—Frank Hinton, author of *Action, Figure*

"In his brilliantly imaginative and allegorical collection of linked pieces, Mike Kleine explores that which remains standing in the face of human mortality. From Google maps to the pink sky, the hospital waiting room to the moon and tides, Kleine conveys the eternity of nature within a web of impermanence."
—Melissa Broder, author of *Scarecrone*

"*Arafat Mountain* is a sad eternity of pointless deaths and consumerism. A celebration of late capitalism in decline—dressed in animal skins and death. You will gnash your teeth and tear at your eyes and fill your mouth with charcoal and paper clips."
—Ofelia Hunt, author of *Today & Tomorrow*

"Inject Kanye West with cosmological prowess and the desire to kill, and he just might write *Arafat Mountain*. This is one weird guide to the inner fashions of the violent rich."
—Ken Baumann, author of *Solip*

"Come to no decisions. Expect nothing in particular. Expect anything. Expect everything. This is not an object you are holding. *Arafat Mountain* is a hole—like being in a light-speed car, where everything is super bright, a beautiful blur, but then the car stops for a brief moment and suddenly, you can see everything, before shooting away again at the speed of light. The parallel universes in this book exist, not so that Mike, or the reader, can explore the idea of parallel universes, but rather, to make it clear that with this book, it is permissible to inhabit a parallel universe. You, the reader, can create your own parallel universe, your own sense of fashion, your own gods. This book—for me— was a lesson in meaninglessness. Any attempt to settle upon a final approach was meaningless. And what makes this book so powerful is the fact that you actually *can* feel here, in what you read, what you aren't reading. This book will startle you. It will startle you every time you pick it up."
—Ken Sparling, author of *Intention Implication Wind*

Also by Mike Kleine

Mastodon Farm

Ararat
MOUNTAIN
MIKE KLEINE

ATLATL

Yellow Springs, OH

Arafat Mountain
First Edition

ISBN-13: 978-1-941918-03-06
ISBN-10: 1941918034

Printed in the United States of America.

Cover Design & Illustrations by Austin Breed
Author Photo Collage by Nate James
Book Design by Mike Kleine & Andersen Prunty
Author Photo by Courtney Moore

For my mother, naturally

The earth makes a sound as of sighs and the last drops fall from the emptied cloudless sky. A small boy, stretching out his hands and looking up at the blue sky, [asks] his mother how such a thing [is] possible. Fuck off, she [says].

—Samuel Beckett

In order to understand the world, one has to turn away from it on occasion.

—Albert Camus

Ararat Mountain

MIKE KLEINE

ATLATL
Yellow Springs, OH

We jump from the mouth of the helicopter. A few of us don't make it. We walk toward Arafat Mountain. Davis decides, at some point, "I want to stay behind." At the castle, a taxi waits. Nearby, there is a hotel with a golf course, five horses and a red Ferrari. Luc says to the taxi driver, "Take us to the mountains." We drive up to the mountains in the taxicab toward a château that is painted white. Amir and Raymond and Camille and Marc and François follow with the horses. Majeed crashes the Ferrari on the side of Arafat Mountain. We never see him again. Benoit says to Emili, "Look, even more mountains—behind that really big one over there." Of course, Benoit is talking about Arafat Mountain. The taxi driver says, "After the earthquakes, the white men stayed and most of the black population fled." We stop to look at Arafat Mountain. A plume of white smoke escapes from somewhere near the bottom. We see graffiti. The words *tangerine* and *Malibu* and *night* and *dreams*. Animals and insects. Green moss and dirty skin too. A savage landscape. "This is the place where it happened."

In a parallel universe, Werner Herzog releases the *Grizzly Man* death tape. At Arafat Mountain, a new religion is born: Geodesic Surrealism. Christian lights a joint, takes two hits, and passes it to Michael. Michael takes the joint and pretends to inhale. Christian says, "Don't waste the weed." A couple of black girls leave the city on a Friday evening. They spend the entire weekend in the mountains. They camp out in the woods. The father of one of the girls is a judge so she has a lot of money. The girls play loud rap music. They dance until the end of the night. They keep dancing after the night is over. They don't stop until the following morning. They sleep for a little bit and keep dancing the rest of the next day, because: drugs. The loud music bothers the neighbors, not because it is loud, because they are white. A serial killer—good at cosmic travel and shape-shifting stuff—wanders into the mountains and through the woods. The serial killer sees the cabin. He hears the music. He sets the cabin on fire. The girls don't make it. A neighbor spots the serial killer. "Hey, I'll pay you $100 if you kill some more girls." The serial killer accepts the money. Pinkerton says, "This paint is not the same paint I used last year." The suitcase Debra takes on her trip is not very heavy but looks super nice. "Louis Vuitton." Teddy Hoover loses his shoe during the home invasion. The lawyer says something to the judge about Gérard and Gérard thinks about how hot it is outside right now. Amanda says, "This just isn't the same beach house as last year—it can't be." Peter says, "Baby, I had to downsize."

A black hole finds ~~god~~ and eats ~~him~~. After that,
Arafat Mountain.

They arrive at Arafat Mountain. Joffrey yells something. Space rock falls from the sky. They bury Dave near the tomb of Amuul'Dh'arrah and spend the rest of the day looking for the Multidimensional Space Particle. They cannot find it. Zodiac asks Salaam'Am'Salaam if he believes the Multidimensional Space Particle is real. "No, I do not believe the Multidimensional Space Particle exists. It is a peradam." After a while, Joffrey perishes and the body is thrown into a caldera. They say a few prayers and—at the same time— Zodiac realizes it is very cold on top of Arafat Mountain. They fall asleep and dream of beds made of glass and marble. Of planets designed by Jean Paul Gaultier and galaxies rendered by Ralph Lauren. In a different dream, Zodiac and Salaam'Am'Salaam travel to the skies with Shamraat'Dean—~~god~~ of suicides and cosmic violence—in search of abandoned wormholes, pataphysical tribes and spacetime stuff. Zodiac imagines the face of Joffrey in the shape of the moon. He thinks he sees Elaj'uaan too. Zodiac has a fourth dream that same night but forgets what it is by morning.

"Fuck."

They spend the weekend eating lobster. Paulin forgets he is allergic to shellfish. Nobody attempts to save him because no one is a doctor. They go outside to the yard to bury Paulin. They take their time because they know: Paulin isn't going anywhere. Antoine says, "I hate the moon." He thinks about something else. "The lunar landing was a fake and it was done by white people and NASA and Stanley Kubrick." A bird makes the sound of a bird in the sky and they hear the sound of waves. Eugene arrives on a jet ski. He is wearing a Prospekt Supply windbreaker with Opening Ceremony Pojagi Jacquard slim shorts. He walks onto the compound and into the yard and says to no one in particular, "Google Maps saved my life!" The sun is setting and they march into the sea. The sky is brown. In total, they are maybe twenty-nine. A man from the other village arrives. He plays bard songs on bagpipes and sings to make the kids dance, so they can forget, maybe, that Paulin is dead. Eventually, the creature—that thing from the lagoon—comes from out of the sea and takes Paulin's body and disappears, in a mess of cloud and froth and steam and foam. The words *cosmic* and *horror* dance across the sky in the form of yellow lightning with no sound or thunder, just for an instant—with the music of bagpipes and sound of kids—before vanishing, forever, into the never-ending landscape.

They leave on a speedboat. They are in a hurry.
They go to somewhere in Europe, or South
America—Antwerp maybe.

Haruubi-Ma'an Taap stops to stare at ~~his~~ own re-flexion. ~~He~~ stares at the reflexion in the golden blue paleness of the clean Caucasian moonlight. ~~He~~ says, "The sun must rise again." Haruubi-Ma'an Taap murders one of the disciples so they will learn. They take notes. "~~My~~ body is a complete production. A circular cycle. A broken vessel. A gift from the heavens—in alliance with the earth and the moon and the stars and the solar system and the galaxy and everything after that."

They do cartwheels in the grass and ask each other questions about the past. Like: "Who were you before you came to the château?" and, "What were you doing before you came to the château?" and, "Why did you come to the château?"—things like that. Hector is the most interesting. He does a cartwheel and says, "Death squad stuff."

The astrophysicist says something to the slaves about a cosmic mountain somewhere. "There's this cave that's full of mystical creatures. A long-lost artifact from the ancient world—that's hidden treasure stuff too!" He mentions, briefly, a wife and three-year old daughter. "I've finally found the solution to our problem though—I think." The astrophysicist leaves on a speedboat. "I'll be back. Soon, I promise." He looks up into the purple-blue sky and lies to himself. He never returns; not even after one-hundred million years.

Eric is late on paying rent. Zodiac says to Imhotep, Eric's landlord, "Imhotep, because Eric is already late on paying rent for his apartment, why don't we take him to the forest and hunt him in teams?" A few hours pass. Zodiac and Imhotep and a small group of very exclusive friends go out. They travel into the forest and they hunt.

The apartment was in a convenient location—a beautiful part of the neighborhood—with access to Broadway, Central Park, Times Square; all that. Apartment 2B. This was where Barry and Nora lived. Barry and Nora had been living together for a little over thirteen months. Last Tuesday was when Barry made the decision, finally, to purchase a brand new television for the both of them—Barry and Nora—but more for Nora. That evening, Barry took the F train after work to a Best Buy to compare different models of television sets he had seen in the newspaper ad and it wasn't until after a little while (fifty minutes to be exact) that Barry realized the store did not carry many—or any—of the models of television sets he had seen in the ad. "That's because this is out of date," one of the salespersons said to Barry, about the ad. "Out of date?" Barry said. "If you look here," the salesperson said, pointing to something in the ad, "this is an ad from October of last year. Now, our televisions are much bigger and certainly, much better." All of this information came as a sudden flash of light—a revelation, if you will—to Barry and for a quick moment, Barry felt overwhelmed, his brain: heavy, for it wasn't in Barry's habits normally, to check the date on old newspaper ads. But Barry recuperated (from this malaise) rather promptly and went along with most of what the salesperson had to say and in the end, decided, finally, to purchase the most recent high definition Panasonic television set they had available and said to the salesperson, "Thanks. Nora will really love this." But Barry could feel that maybe—in the end—he would be more excited than Nora, about the new television set. But Barry was okay with that. And he still continued with the original plan, in his head, when he arrived home and said, "Surprise," to Nora, and showed her the box. On the box were words like: studio master panel and built-in wi-fi and incredible invisible speaker system and trend-setting 95,000:1 dynamic contrast ratio and single ISFccct compression cable of professional calibration for optimum picture quality and performance and 1080p and full HD and 3 HDMI plug-ins and 1.3 digital input (for the PC). Barry knew Nora liked to watch movies on the television. She liked to turn the volume up very loud. Barry also knew the apartment downstairs had been left vacant by its previous owners for almost two weeks (and would remain that way for another three, he would be told later by the landlady) so Barry thought, *this is perfect timing* and *Nora deserves this*. And since this night was one that was much like any other—a Tuesday, in fact—the high definition 60-inch Panasonic television set with its studio master panel and built-in wi-fi and incredible invisible speaker system and trend-setting 95,000:1 dynamic contrast ratio and single ISFccct compression cable of professional calibration for optimum picture quality and performance and 1080p and full HD and 3 HDMI plug-ins and 1.3 digital input (for the PC) was playing very loudly. And Nora was happy. Barry could see that. But no one heard the doorbell the first time. (Although, it must be said; Barry thought he heard something at first, but then considered that maybe, his mind was playing tricks on him (again) and that what he thought he heard, was actually imagined and ultimately, a consequence, and combination, of: hard work, a long week, and very little sleep). The high definition Panasonic television set said something about people dying in Venezuela and something else about a record heat-wave happening somewhere in Europe, but the entire time, Barry thought, *I'm just glad Nora is happy right now*. And then the words *terrible lies* and *broken promises* flashed in front of Barry's eyes and what he thought might be the migraines again, quickly dissipated and turned, instead, into terrible thoughts and visions, like: *why can't I be more successful* and *what if I die tomorrow* and the image of Barry tumbling and falling—all bloodied and bruised—down the side of a mountain somewhere in Brazil. This went on for maybe a minute. And because of this, Barry began to sweat. Then the doorbell rang, a second time. And Barry snapped out of it, and this time, was sure he had heard something; so he stood up and turned the volume down on the high definition Panasonic television set and looked at Nora. Nora said, "Where are you going?" Barry said, "Did you hear something?" Barry turned around and looked at the door and naturally, the door did nothing. "What'd you say," Nora said, finally. She stared at Barry. Barry still looked at the door. "The door," Barry said, pointing at the door. "Someone just rang the doorbell." Nora, in turn, looked at the door, saw nothing, and again—much like had happened for Barry—the door, also, did nothing. "Yeah, isn't it too late for that, or something," Nora said, to Barry. Barry looked at Nora and shrugged. Nora looked at the numbers on the Mediacom digital cable box and saw the time and said, "It's past midnight already." And Barry looked at Nora and said, "Yeah." When the doorbell rang a third time, Barry jumped a little—and this, mostly because he didn't expect a third ring but also, because Barry generally didn't like surprises, and this third ring, of all things, was most certainly a surprise, especially at this time of night. So Barry turned to look at Nora. The volume on the high definition Panasonic television set was still turned down, and now, on the television screen, a movie was playing: a confusing car chase. Cars kept changing colors in hyperactive errors of continuity and a man in a white robe was being chased, in slow motion, by a woman in a blue dress and the words *DRACULA* and *BLACK* kept flashing in big giallo letters on the television screen. What the high definition Panasonic television set did not show, however, and maybe unfortunately, was something about the killer— or, Zodiac (the man with the face of a moon)—at the door. And during all of this, Nora thought about stuff, like: *quantum physics, space shuttles exploding, the ozone, the number of pancakes she had eaten since January, nudist colonies, ultra-violence, the color purple, motorcycle gangs in Russia, post-modern essays, Dochevsky, all the people in Japan, Arafat Mountain, time travel, sunlight from the moon* and *fucking*. Nora thought about *fucking* a lot. The words *perfect daughter* and *surrogate mother* flashed across her brain and Nora smiled. In a more perfect universe, Barry would have hugged Nora and consoled her and said, "Everything is going to be all right," and then opened the door; but this was not *that* universe. In this universe, Barry thought of tomorrow—and all the other tomorrows after that—and turned the lock, and scratched his left arm a little with his right hand and opened the door.

In outer space. 'Also Sprach Zarasthura' by
Richard Strauss. Then gladiators and Vietnam
bullets. After a while—silence. Here, everything
moves in super slow motion. Even the birds.

After Arafat Mountain. Night time. At the place, where the earthquake happened. A thin man. Misaki. The young reporter. Charanjit Singh. In the upstairs dining room. By himself. "Now is a good time, actually, the best time, probably, to interview." Upstairs. Yellow lights. A meteor. Music. *Quiet*. Orange: everything. Charanjit Singh, smiling. Interpreter, "From Mauritius." "All of this, it's very bad." "People never forget." Explosion. Smoke. Cigarettes. Words on paper. Ten minutes. Dead limo drivers. Everything happening. At the same time. Downstairs. The Return of Misaki. A bottle of sake. A middle-aged woman, this time. A digital voice recorder. And her hand. A failed marriage. "I write for a very famous music magazine." Her real name. Seven minutes. Another meteor. "I will never forget who you are." An earthquake. Again. Arafat Mountain. Interpreter from Mauritius. Another explosion. Downstairs. The thin man. "I now

understand everything, yes." "Everything cannot
be undone." Seven billion broken bodies. And a
taxicab, yellow. The road to the office. No sound
yet. The red sky. Clouds. Night time, still.
Shadows, somewhere. Something, up there.
Arafat Mountain. All over. Again.

Heaven is Arafat Mountain.

The following morning—at the place with the hotel—during a tournament of golf, the earth begins to tremble. The oceans overflow and space rock falls from out of the sky. Bernard becomes pulverized. The way he looks—he looks like hamburger meat. The original owner of the château flees—in his speedboat. He escapes the island in a hurry. He does not want to become pulverized by the space rock. He says, "Enough with all these space rocks falling from the sky!" Thierry somersaults into a shallow ravine and avoids becoming pulverized. He ruins his Marc by Marc Jacobs charcoal grey minimalist trousers but is relieved. He grabs the body of Bernard and says, "Once this is all over, I think we need to bury Bernard; his body. Somewhere in the gardens. Somewhere nice." He points to some flowers. "Bernard was not a good man." Omar—on the other side—sinks a 55-foot eagle putt. They halt the game because of cosmic vibrations. The gardener comes and says, "M. Antoine believes it is no longer safe for you out here on the green with all this falling space rock." He motions to some of the space rock on the ground and looks up into the orange-blue sky and back at the men playing golf—as if to say, "You are all fucking crazy for playing golf out here, right now." Instead, though, he says, "If you come back to the château, where it will be more safe for you, there is a surprise." Back at the château, there are white women and plenty of slaves. This is the surprise. Jacques kills one of the women and her friend screams. A servant executes her.

A breezy Sunday afternoon on a beach, in July, somewhere behind Arafat Mountain, near the middle of the day. A family from Europe enjoying a picnic on the side of a cliff. 'Lumpumgu' by Kankolongo Alidor and Kayoka Ladistas playing on the transistor radio. At first, a sound. Then, a meteor rips through the breezy-blue sky. Mark, who is fifteen years old, notices and says, (to no one is particular, probably more to himself) "Is this the end of the world?" Martha (the mother) says nothing at all (because she cannot hear Mark), and turns the volume down on the transistor radio to say, "What?" Tom, the father, scratches his head and says, "Of course not." He stands and walks over to where Mark (the son) is sitting and (sits, also, and) puts one arm around Mark (to comfort him) and says, "The end of the world is not a real thing." Martha smiles and stands (also) and walks over to where Tom is sitting (by Mark) and rubs Mark on the head and touches Tom on the shoulder because, she thinks, *Tom is a good father and a loyal husband* and *Mark is a fantastique son* and *I am happy, very happy right now, yes ...(and this is the apocalypse)*. Mark shrugs and looks at Martha (who is now looking at Tom), and smiles and thinks, *I am very young* and *none of this matters anyway* and *by the time I care about any of this, we will all be dead and gone*, and rolls over and picks up the 925-page hardcover copy of *IQ84* by Haruki Murakami from the grass that Tom checked out (for him) from the bibliothèque late Friday evening (after work) and resumes reading 'Part I, Chapter 15, Aomame: Firmly, Like Attaching an Anchor to a Balloon'. Tom looks at Mark and whispers something to Martha and then looks up into the cosmos and thinks, *Maybe the world really is coming to an end; the kingdom, it really is coming.*

Martin asks Jean-Phillipe about the lever in the
media room and Jean-Phillipe says, "Never touch
the lever in the media room."

Words begin to appear in the cornflower blue sky
and somewhere far far way—in the Tucana Dwarf
Galaxy—a woman kills herself.

Flat says in a weird voice that doesn't sound like Flat, "I guess I'm stuck in this castle right now, with these other people, for a little while. Here, actually, they call it a château. And the shaman, he's from outer space." Then he says, "Is this Flat? I don't know you, maybe? Send me the address so I can meet you." Hong goes to get a pen and piece of paper so he can maybe write the address of this place where Flat is staying. He wants to go there. But the address is wrong, or, he isn't able to find it on Google Maps. At the airport, he shows it to the lady behind the counter and she says, "Twelve thousand dollars." An hour later, Hong is on a speedboat with Israel, and they are somewhere near Arafat Mountain and the château.

Patrice takes them hunting. They go into the forest riding stallions. It is warm outside. The birds move like black glue. They shoot quail, duck and pheasant. They go back to the castle. Yolande is not there. She has left and gone to some other place that is more safe. On the coffee table, a note, in easy-to-read cursive. "Yolande, who will be gone for one-hundred thousand years, is on vacation to Antigua." They do not know how to cook quail. They do not know how to cook duck or pheasant. They say a quick prayer and leave the birds on the front lawn, for the animals.

The stomach of the volcano and the elevator that
goes to the moon.

Arafat Mountain is Hell.

Zodiac watches a PBS documentary. The man on the television discusses earth magic, hauntology and cosmology. He says a few things about quantum physics and apocalyptic beach parties in Guadalajara and mentions the online website Wikipedia. Another man with red hair says some things about hyperspace and mysticism. He mentions pop art and the ancients. Zodiac thinks, *the ancients*. There is a brief segment on cosmic caverns and ruined cities; Geodesic Surrealism and the history of Tikrit; interconnectedness and Middle Egyptian hieroglyphics; demiurges and *l'esprit d'escalier*. Niel deGrasse Tyson shows up and discusses quantum vibes and string theory; pirate radio stations in Antarctica and combinatory aesthetics. Zodiac flips the channel and a woman is quickly explaining the importance of leisure safaris to an Asmat tribe in Africa. Zodiac thinks, *the ancients*. There is a diagram on the screen describing holotropic breathwork and the Yucca Mountain slipstream. A few minutes pass and a different, but still fairly young-looking lady, discusses Gnostic Realism and individualized awareness; fluid particles and multidimensional rifts; time warps and extraterrestrials; the Fibonacci sequence and parallel universes. The final segment—narrated by some cheap Bill Nye look-a-like—covers CP-Symmetry and the tenth dimension.

At the hotel party, Basille meets a woman from a Type III civilization and says, "The lever in the media room—it does cosmic things and I do not understand."

Sometimes, Hector will break character and say all the wrong things. Like this one time, when he turned down the volume on the television set and said to Rian, "The blood is coming, I think."

Somewhere in Andalusia, Derrick has a Technicolor dream. In his dream, Arthur stands tall and stalls. Then, he walks straight into the Caspian Sea. His body sizzles. The skin falls from off his back. The muscles burn. The sky turns a fuzzy wuzzy burning green. The music plays louder. You can even see the bone. Everything turning red hot. Smoke everywhere. Then Arthur screams. Derrick screams. Zodiac screams. Martha screams. And in the room next door—where the audience is sitting and waiting and watching—the real Arthur wakes up and screams. Then he does another dream.

Adam says, "Go to the mountain." He points to a direction, vaguely. "It is waiting, there, for you. It is not going anywhere. *I* am here to stay. *The mountain*, there, it is there to stay too. It is not moving—not soon anyway. Arafat Mountain." "I am not leaving here. You are alone, I cannot do that. Go and leave you here. No. Not without anyone." "I am not alone. I am someone. Anyone, here, is me. I am here." "You are here but who else is here with you? I can see only you. And no one else. You are alone and I do not see anyone else. No one else is here with you but me." "I am someone. So no one is false. There is someone here, in this room. Right now. You leave me here for one hundred years and come back, you will find my remains. They will say, *who was this man*, and they will do some tests and take a sample from my bones and use a technology—something from the future—to determine who I am. And they will say, *ah, yes, he is someone.*

And someone else will say, *he was someone.* So, you see? I am someone. Don't insult me. Please, go. I am not alone. I am fine. Here in the now. This is *me.*"

Wednesday. Georges leaves a very long voice mail detailing the capture of Khonsu-Ma'an-Taap (~~god~~ of the moon) and Bes-Ta'am'Riip (~~god~~ of the cosmos).

Early one morning, Dr. Caligulua enters a village and conducts a thought experiment. He sends a poor woman to the 9th dimension.

From the observatory, they watch at night, for stars. Al-Sham'raat-Al'Dean, ~~god~~ of teleportation and cosmic integrity disintegrates. A scientist from the laboratory upstairs: "We have finally figured it out—how to create the Sub Quantum Unified Intrinsic Field Device." After the dry cleaners and fast food, Imperial Wizard opens a few duffel bags. "Givenchy. Christian Dior, Gucci, Prada, Calvin Klein. And this one, Gosha Rubchinskiy." The room with the lever—on the first floor. "Before the end of each day— whenever, whomever—just pull the lever." Owen pulls the lever after the first day, only. And that's it. The boys—Damien, Dennis, Eugene, Flat, Henri, Marion, Timor and Rian—they all walk toward the salty ocean. Hand-in-hand. Stuck in a loop. Forever. No remorse. Joan presses her face to the edge of the end of the world, and feels the coolness of the dirt—as it rises and escapes into her pores—through the balaclava. Caleb jumps from a seventeen story condo. Five minutes later, the moon melts. A unicorn, tangled in the windbreak tree. Brother Cyst   and Sister Creature. Space pirates and strange noises from the cosmos.

A pleasant, warm, quiet Sunday afternoon on the countryside somewhere near Arafat Mountain. Music playing from somewhere in the sky. It is the year of Salaam'Am'Salaam. Zodiac makes an oath to Elajou-An-Inkh-Tah, ~~god~~ of deception and greed. He imagines space rockets to Saturn and conversations with aliens about the world coming to an end. Zodiac unrolls his prayer mat and walks outside into the grass and faces Equi-All-Sal'aad. Zodiac looks up into the blue-black sky and feels the energy of the cosmos. *I LIKE KILLING PEOPLE BECAUSE IT IS SO MUCH FUN IT IS MORE FUN THAN KILLING WILD GAME IN THE FORREST BECAUSE MAN IS THE MOST DANGEROUS ANIMAL OF ALL TO KILL SOMETHING GIVES ME THE MOST THRILLING EXPERIENCE IT IS EVEN BETTER THAN GETTING YOUR ROCKS OFF WITH A GIRL THE BEST PART OF IT IS THAT WHEN I DIE I WILL BE REBORN IN PARADISE AND THE ONES I*

HAVE KILLED WILL BECOME MY SLAVES I WILL NOT GIVE YOU MY NAME BECAUSE YOU WILL TRY TO SLOW ME DOWN OR STOP MY COLLECTING OF SLAVES FOR MY AFTER LIFE EBEORIETEMETHHPITI. He continues this prayer for seventeen hours.

"I meet the hero pit bee / I meet the Hopie tribe / I'm the pitee / Brother Pete II / Timothy Peter Biehe. / Timothie Peter Beihe / He Be Timothie I Peter. / I'm The Teepie Brother / I'm The Piteee Brother / Be(fe)ore I Meet The Pith / Eerie Tomb Hi The Piet / Timothie Peter Beihe / Poet Here Tie Bite Him."

~~Mother~~ is bleeding from somewhere on ~~her~~ face. ~~She~~ says, "~~I~~ was tied to a chair. They shot her. In the brain. The two men. The two men with masks. She will never be the same."

The mountain sleeps.

Luc discovers the body of Israel on a Wednesday morning underneath the tarp of the south estate swimming pool. The water in the swimming pool begins to boil. Luc ignores the smell. He says to M. Antoine, "He was completely full of water and bloated and ballooning, still, when I found him." M. Antoine tells us he will conduct an investigation with a detective—a true detective—from France, to look into Israel's death, since there is the possibility of a murder made to look like a suicide. M. Antoine says, "I will hire the best coroner to look into Israel's death. Spare no expense, for Israel was my friend." The coroner comes later that evening. A man with thinning grey hair. He says, "It's in the ground, the vibrations. Can you feel them? Like they're coming for you."

He takes us to the study for drinks and opens a picture book and says, "Here they are, my prized possessions," and points to names. "Theresa (an oncologist,) Jean-Pierre (a vagrant,) Damien (a demonologist,) Jacques (a language professor from Brussels,) Isabelle (a socialite,) Chadwick (a professional organizer,) Brian (a Jesuit,) Carissa (a watchmaker from Hawa'ii,) Shandi (a book reader,) Symone (a model,) Gérard (a homosexual,) Adrianna (a lobster enthusiast,) Mao Mao (an island dictator,) Travis (a pessimist,) Anaïs (a perfumier,) Lawrence (a nuclear physicist,) Victor (a tennis player,) Liz (a graffiti artist from LA,) Christian (a college professor at Harvard,) Arron (a mathematician,) Elsie (a modern artist,) Lesha (a jetsetter,) Arthur (an ethical subjectivist,) Johnny (a man from Madrid,) Harrison (a Geodesic Surrealist,) Freeman (a theoretical physicist,) Beverly (a child actor,) Jenna (a banker,) Phil (a teacher,)

Minerva (an astrophysicist,) Adam (a crystal healer,) Diggins (a quasi-realist,) Inida (a media mogul,) Azamat (a radical,) Manuel (an apprentice,) Kevin (a health product spokesperson,) Jaysson (a pacifist,) Gomez (a painter from Antigua,) Thessalonian (a marriage counselor,) Bloom (a substance abuse counselor,) Ozymandias (a mesmerist,) Marty (a womanizer,) Beth (a television news anchor,) Temple (a marine biologist,) Flat (a music producer,) Pat (a chemist,) Ken (a wholesaler,) Anoesia (a chief school administrator,) Guillermo (a convict,) Maria (a metaphysician,) Hannibal (a historian,) Charles (a con artist,) Dedalus (a phlebotomist,) Algernon (a bird watcher,) Pippa (a deity,) Quentin (a primatologist,) Thierry (a parapsychologist,) Ingrid (an illusionist,) Kyle (a pornographer,) Merlin (a deontologist,) Terrence (an ethnobotanist,) Mabel (an electric car enthusiast,) Sophie (an ideologist,) Tammy (a bartender,) Nic (a family man,) Glen (a paleontologist,) Al-Sayeer (a Sheik from the United Arab Emirates,) Henri (a boy,) David (an island caretaker,) Julianne (an astronomer from France,) Robert (a white hat hacker,) Tara (a masseuse,) Lord Langston (a Holocaust sympathizer,) Mayneard (a Satanist,) Izzy (a shooting party connoisseur,) Janey (a researcher at the Institute of Extraspatial Studies,) Marion (a hedonist,) Emma (a damaged poet,) Paul (a bounty hunter,) Gwen (a social worker,) Jill (an embalmer,) Standard (a Gnostic philosopher,) Atticus (a playwright,) Kendrick (a rapper,) Alan (a consultant,) Tim (a warlock) Pat (a psychonaut,) Lionel (a linguist,) Yorrick (a hot dog vendor,) Alton (a moral realist,) Evian (a body part model,) Al (a live mannequin,) Everett (a cruise ship entertainer,) Addesyn (a famous actor,) Bradley Hoover (a civil engineer,) Israel (an ophthalmologist,) Cohle (a biker skinhead,) Gabriel (a genetic counselor,) Zaïda (a pearl diver,) Danica (a museum enthusiast,) Ivan (a submarine cook,) Dhvnvnjvy (the first,) Delma (a voice actor,) Donn (an ocularist,) Mme Claude (a psychic,) Roy (a foley artist,) Samuel (a descendant,) Hilary (a librarian,) Molly (an equestrian,) Everett (a sommelier,) Powell (a soil conservationist,) Evan (a Chief Executive Officer,) Caryl (a film maker,) Tito (a book editor,) Patsy (a singer,) Oswald (a former Hitler Youth,) Robert (an oral surgeon,) Ernst (a German music critic,) Yianne (a priest,) Denise (a school teacher,) Ruth (a stunt double,) Gregory (a therapist) and Michael (a writer)." He drinks from the glass and knocks the whiskey stones against his teeth. "These are my slaves. *Enchanté.*"

Abduul Amrahh-To'oul attempts to escape during the middle of the night. Fritz, the German Shepherd from Germany, thinks otherwise, and tears ~~him~~ to pieces.

She is the Wandering Wolf. "We are the cum of the earth." The inside of the mountain is made to look like a video game. "Terrence drives the 2003 Chevy Impala with a sexy ass." Blue lights and sleek contours with music everywhere. Everything from the 80s. Red race stripes. S/he says some things about ~~gods~~ and prayer and living forever—disappearing into freedom.

The summer is thick with heatwaves and this terrible gooey humidity. As if the ~~gods~~ are angry at us—the world. Jeffrey succumbs to the drought and we drive the body into town—with the AC on full blast—and ask for directions to the ancient burial place of Mocatesh'Sayeer. We fall upon a man harvesting what he calls, "The fallen stars of our generation." We hear the sound of something illegal—a street race— happening somewhere in the mountains. *Suicide Mountain XIII.*

Mr. Mahmoud on the beach at night. Black stars and everything. Waves making the sound of waves. Mr. Mahmoud thinks about the beach and the sand and the night. Everything around him. The quiet. How, at night, the beach looks nothing like the beach during the day. Mostly, because the people are missing. But also, because it is dark. Moreover, Mr. Mahmoud, also, is not in the habit of standing on the beach at night, in the middle of the summer, in the darkness. In Mr. Mahmoud's head, the people and the umbrellas—this is what he associates to the beach. And at night, the beach is something that becomes a dark and unfamiliar place. A scary thing. Almost like the invisible monster. *Abject.* But Mr. Mahmoud moves closer to the sound of waves. He is wearing loafers. And he knows, absolutely, that eventually, the waves will touch his shoes and make them become wet. But he moves up closer, still, Mr. Mahmoud, toward the sound of waves. And the sound of waves becomes louder. More clear. And because it is night and it is dark, Mr. Mahmoud is not sure when his shoes are going to become wet. But it is an inevitability that he must experience, he feels. Mr. Mahmoud. It is something that is necessary—that needs to happen. On the beach. At night. In the middle of the summer. Where it is dark. But there are lights too, off in the distance. Mr. Mahmoud is unsure about the lights. Their origin. Mr. Mahmoud isn't sure if the lights are from a boat, or a man who is stranded in the middle of the ocean, or a floating lighthouse, or a fishing ship of sorts, or some new type of sea creature or animal, or monster, or if it is merely an illusion, something that is in his head, a giant diamond in the middle of the ocean, a reflexion of the moon atop the water, a submarine, the ruins of a lost civilization, a piece of glass from the bottom of the ocean, a barrel of toxic waste, fiber optic cables that have to do with the Internet or some type of mystical creature from deep down or an angel from the Heavens or something like that—perhaps a merman from within. Mr. Mahmoud thinks about the merman. Mr. Mahmoud thinks about the origin of the light, how far away it is. Yet, the longer he stares at it, the closer it seems to where he is standing. Mr. Mahmoud looks around, to see if anyone else is around, looking at him. But it is hard to see anyone. The moon is not out, Mr. Mahmoud realizes, after a bit. So the light off in the distance is not from the moon. It cannot be. But still, Mr. Mahmoud is fascinated by the light and what it means, really, to his life. And also, the absence of the moon. What does *that* mean? Mr. Mahmoud thinks about a world without the moon. He thinks about grade school. Science class. The teacher who once said the moon controls the tides. And how, if there is no moon, oceans will no longer be under control and the water will just go everywhere. Mr. Mahmoud decides the moon is something that has value and thinks, *how much value*? Mr. Mahmoud thinks about the moon some more and feels immediately, *cosmic horror.*

We open Google Maps. We search for life on other planets. We search for Arafat Mountain. Then we search for palm trees and things like that.

Like Robinson Crusoe on his island, Mary burns forest fires at night. She dances witch dances during the day, and sits quietly sometimes, looking into the night sky. The slanting blue. Contemplating. Reflecting. Thinking. About Carcosa Island. Her time in college. Things she has done. Stuff she has seen. Mary thinks about the time she was a family. What she is doing now. She remembers names, like: Todd, Eric, Cartier, Evan, Gavin, Terrence, Jim, Adam, Zach, Hector, Emma, Elen, Tamara, Alicia, Hank, Umberto, Justin and Yasmine. But she can't remember faces. She avoids those she loves. And disregards enemies too. Mary. Alone. The island. Like Robinson Crusoe. With no one at her side. Forever.

Sharp notes and hi-hats.

Proust is the second gardener. The gardener who works during the evenings. This is his third job. He has been working on these grounds the last eighteen years. Last weekend, he went mental and killed eleven island people. It made national news and several reporters tried to get interviews but they kept telling the reporters, "This isn't even *our* château." They tried calling the owners after the incident. It didn't work because they were unable to find a good signal at the château. They even went outside, to the flattest part of the roof—but that was something about the château: terrible *terrible* cell phone reception, anywhere, in any room: everywhere. Even with Verizon, Zodiac was unable to get any bars. Phillipe had Sprint. Phillipe, sometimes, was able to get maybe, one or two bars, but most times, even on a good day, Phillipe had none, usually.

The screen flashes for a second. Zodiac is thinking about a woman who is tired. Somewhere near Arafat Mountain, a woman is tired and she is wearing a white dress. She is burning fires. The dress is her costume. Normally, this dress would function as a symbol for her kindness and feminine virtue (or something) but in reality, this woman is neither kind nor virtuous. She is tired. She is evil. And she's a good guy. So it's okay. At this moment in the film, the woman is gracefully sauntering down a brightly lit staircase holding what appears to be a shotgun. Her dress is covered in blood. She has just survived a violent attack. An ambush of sorts. They're all dead and she's not. She's fine. This is important because she is a female actress playing the role of the lead male character. The good guy. In this story, she is the good guy and the good guy has just survived an ultraviolent fight scene. The violence is over-the-top. This is the scene that was shot in one continuous take. Impressive. Now the floor is slippery. A film critic might describe the fifteen-minute fight sequence as somewhat epic or even quasi-operatic. "Bursting with style and over-the-top violence, acclaimed filmmaker Zodiac's latest offering, reads like an action flick but plays like a love story." "Imagine Joan Crawford and Uma Thurman as one person. The brave lead female character of this story: the tired woman in the white dress." "Brilliant cinema," a newspaper ad will claim. "A must see," Roger Ebert will say, "terribly engrossing." Zodiac will make sure to perfect the long-shot technique so that his film will be considered *art house* by popular film festivals, like Sundance. *The* mise-en-scène *will need to be impeccable*, Zodiac thinks. *Impeccable.* As she descends, gore dominates the décor. The tired woman clearly won this battle. Nobody stood a chance. Nobody ever stands a chance. In a tightly cropped close-up, we can see that she is also holding a pair of scissors in her right hand. She is using both the thumb and right index finger to hold the scissors in place. She makes a cutting motion with them after each step. The scissors drip with fluids. As she descends, the camera slowly zooms out to reveal a bloodied arena, now displaying the results of even more random acts of violence. This is Zodiac's directorial debut. She wants this scene to be perfect. Zodiac wants this scene to be perfect. It doesn't feel natural though. The actress playing the tired woman is taking her time going down the staircase because she is trying to make sure she doesn't trip and fall but she is also taking her time because she wants to make sure the scene is perfect. This is a pivotal scene in the film. This is the one where she finally speaks with the bad guy. It needs to be perfect. Zodiac begins to create some sort of back story for her character. *Something strange must have happened to her,* Zodiac thinks. *Something bad.* Zodiac decides this film will need to be a film with very little dialogue. *She needs to be unique, Zodiac thinks. Like one of those silent-hero types. The kind you find in Westerns.* After a bit, the character of the tired woman reaches the bottom of the staircase. The woman, who is clearly middle-aged, says something inaudible. She looks into the camera. The music in this particular scene is non-diegetic, so her character cannot hear it but the audience is aware of music playing, somewhere. Again, she says something slightly inaudible, but this time we hear a final vowel and consonant hit the speakers right before the music stops. She stares into the camera. The music stops because Zodiac wants the audience to realize that the music, up to this point, has actually been non-diegetic. Her stare breaks the fourth wall. The audience gasps. This demonstrates the woman's dominating power within the cinematic realm of this film. Her female presence dominates the male-controlled space of the manor. She is in control of the cinematic apparatus. She is bigger than the film crew. Off-screen, she barks orders at the director. Zodiac wants the audience to know that the woman is in control whenever she uses her voice. She hardly ever uses her voice. Zodiac also decides that this is a pivotal scene in the film since she is finally meeting the bad guy. It needs to be perfect. She says something to someone who is off-screen. "It wasn't easy finding you," she says. "How did you get in here," an off-screen voice says. "I used my imagination," she says. The scene closes as the tired woman looks into the camera for the third time and for a brief moment, the screen flickers. This time, she breaks the fifth wall. In the movies, the bad guys always love to talk. So Zodiac decides to switch it up a little. Zodiac decides he wants to develop a bad guy. A memorable sort of bad guy. A bad guy he can maybe use for some other film project. Maybe. So this one is a film about good guys and evil masterminds. The tired woman in the white dress is the good guy. Zodiac thinks about the bad guy for a second. *This one will be some sort of ultraviolent romance,* he thinks, *between the good guy and the bad guy. So now, there also needs to be a lot of dialogue.* Zodiac thinks about what he said before. The bad guy will spend a great deal of time conversing with the main character, the tired woman, before attempting to kill her. This is how the film will end. *Yeah*, Zodiac thinks. *The speech is a very important thing for the bad guy.* For the bad guy, the speech he gives to the good guy, the one where he reveals how he managed to pull off his crime, always serves as exposition for the character of the bad guy. It is during his speech that we, as the audience, learn to sympathize with the bad guy. Or not. "The bad guy will become likable," Zodiac says. "Or not." So Zodiac thinks about a film where the bad guy actually kills the good guy in the end, instead of talking about killing him the entire time. In some mansion, hidden amongst the mountains, the bad guy is a bald man with some form of facial scarring. He's evil because he's never been any good at being nice. Assuming this is the type of film where the good guy is constantly chasing after the bad guy, Zodiac assumes the bad guy doesn't have to worry about real-life things like paying his taxes on time, concealing his identity from the police or actually securing a secret location for his dastardly operations. This world has its own rules and, clearly, this is the type of film where *suspension of disbelief* is essential. This is the type of film where the bad guy is some sort of evil mastermind with a team of henchmen. The henchmen all wear matching suits and the evil mastermind wears an outfit similar to theirs. The difference is, he doesn't look disposable. These henchmen all live within the mansion, yet the location of the mansion is never revealed. *That's director's commentary stuff*, Zodiac thinks. The parodic nature of the film will manifest itself in dozens of self-referential moments to pop culture and other art house type films from the last twenty-seven years or so. The film will not be a success. It will most likely be given an R rating and the excessive use of the word "fuck" will be deemed "unnecessary" by critics. In a parallel universe, Zodiac creates the same film, but this time, the tired woman in the white dress is the bad guy and the man with the facial scar is the good guy. It's PG-13 because the word "fuck" will only be used once. In this version of the film, our bad guy will be captured by the good guy. In a moment of agonizing pain, the bad guy will call the good guy a *motherfucker*. "You're a motherfucker," the bad guy will say in a moment of agonizing pain. The good guy will scratch his ear. Then she will pull some lever, our good guy. The bad guy, the man with the facial scar, will fall to his death in a pit of something dangerous. This will all be shot in one take. This scene will be important. This will be the last part.

Sara shoots Rian in the face. She sits and waits for an hour—until Rian appears again. Rian calls on her cellphone. Sara says, "How are you feeling?" Rian says, "Yeah, I'm outside." Sara says, "Where? In front of the castle?" "No, on the other side." "Did you see the *other* side?" Rian says, "Yes, I saw the other side."

One year: a group of vampires from the south of Spain. They say to the vampires, "Here, the sun is impossible. Life is ~~god~~." They stay for a few days and take pictures of the sky. Before their disappearance, one of them says to Jean-Pierre, something about the year 1967.

On the television, Jacques says to Maude, "If ever, you have the time, please, just kill yourself."

The ground is lava.

Cormac McCarthy releases *Blood Meridian 2*. Tintin falls off the face of a cliff. Saturnin from Kuala Lumpur discovers Gnostic Realism. Basilides the man is banished to 47 Ursae Majoris. Munt'Aal-Piil the god begins his ascent, from the depths of the ocean. Peter Weir explains the ending to *Picnic at Hanging Rock*. In New York City: squid guts, everywhere. 9/11 never happens. Harlan travels back to the time of dinosaurs. Bermuda triangle and four airplanes. A third coming. From the sky: something with sharp teeth and nine eyes. Arthur destroys his Ann De Meulemeester black collection grise trousers. For five minutes, Arafat Mountain disappears. The salt water in the Pacific Ocean begins to boil. Antlers and murder scenes from everywhere. The year 1979. The Napoleon Bonaparte alien microchip. A home planet: destroyed. Anders repeated. Armitage rubble. A cloud in the sky. Disintegration. Oblivion[3].

Barry kisses ~~Bjhjwdmmdxc~~ on the foot and sucks on ~~his~~ big toe. "Nobody's ever done that before," ~~Bcxxhjmwd~~ says. "I know," Barry whispers to ~~Bcxxhjmwd~~. Barry concentrates and alternates between making circles with his tongue and drawing triangles on the tip of ~~Bcxxhjmwd~~'s big toe. ~~Bcxxhjmwd~~ is memorizing Barry's moves because ~~he~~ is thinking ~~he~~ will do the same to Barry's penis once he is done. Barry stops sucking. He moves up. He brushes his left hand through ~~Bcxxhjmwd~~'s hair. Barry follows this move by caressing ~~Bcxxhjmwd~~ on the neck and begins to massage his right shoulder. ~~Bcxxhjmwd~~ makes a sound. "What did you say," Barry says. "Nothing, it just feels really good," ~~Bcxxhjmwd~~ says. "What," Barry says, a second time. *Nevermind*, ~~Bcxxhjmwd~~ thinks. Barry looks ~~Bcxxhjmwd~~ in the eyes. "Nevermind," ~~Bcxxhjmwd~~ says, after about three seconds of awkward silence. Barry wants to keep massaging

Bexxhjmwd's right shoulder but his wrist and forearm are quickly becoming sore. Barry is not in the habit of front shoulder massages. Bexxhjmwd's eyes are closed so Barry does not want to stop. Barry does not want Bexxhjmwd to stare at his face while he is giving him a shoulder massage from the front. *My face is way too close to his face*, Barry thinks. Bexxhjmwd's eyes are still closed. This is the way Barry likes it. It's hard for Barry to look Bexxhjmwd in the eyes because he feels like Bexxhjmwd is judging him whenever he looks into his eyes. Barry looks away because he cannot handle the pressure anymore. He concentrates on a smudge on the wall. *I don't want you to judge me Bexxhjmwd*, Barry thinks. *I'm going to have to work on that, definitely*, Barry thinks. Now, his wrist is getting really sore. Tomorrow, Barry is planning on trying out that new chicken parmesan recipe Krwrdfp gave him. Barry needs his wrist to not be sore if he's going to impress Krwrdfp with that chicken parmesan. Barry leans in and begins to lick Bexxhjmwd's neck. He moans. *Now*, Barry thinks. Barry takes his hand off Bexxhjmwd's shoulder and grabs a hold of his face. They kiss. Bexxhjmwd brushes the contour of Barry's penis with his right hand as they kiss. Barry is wearing a Macy's Private Label dinner jacket over a Marc by Marc Jacobs cotton pique polo, limited edition. The Calvin Klein black slacks beautifully compliment Barry's

Louis Vuitton Explorer sneakers. "I want to rule the earth with you. Like, right now," Bexxhjmwd says with his eyes still closed. "I so want to rule the world with you," Barry says in between kisses, his eyes also closed. Barry says this while taking in Bexxhjmwd's full scent. "Yeah," Bexxhjmwd says. "The world," Barry says. Barry pulls up Bexxhjmwd's skirt and caresses the inside of his right thigh. Barry realizes the warmth of his body is now giving him an erection. He feels like he should take off his Calvin Klein slacks since he does not want to destroy them but he also does not want to ruin the moment with an awkward pause. Barry hates awkward moments. Bexxhjmwd is wearing purple Hello Kitty panties and on the center left there is a wet spot. *That's kind of nasty*, Barry thinks but then closes his eyes. He touches the wet spot with his lips and gives it a big lick. He stares up at Bexxhjmwd who is staring down at him. Bexxhjmwd smiles. Barry moves in again and gives the spot another lick. Now it is really wet. Barry takes off Bexxhjmwd's panties. Bexxhjmwd giggles a little. "Why are you laughing," Barry asks. "Because that tickles," Bexxhjmwd says. Barry doesn't believe Bexxhjmwd. Barry feels like looking at Bexxhjmwd and saying, "Stop," because he no longer is interested in performing oral sex on Bexxhjmwd at this point since he is repulsed by his laugh. Right now, Barry would rather play a quick round of jai alai with ~~Krwrdfp~~. After a bit though, the feeling passes and Barry resumes. Barry licks ~~Bcxxhjmwd~~'s sex. He makes circles and draws triangles with his tongue. "A little more pressure," ~~Bcxxhjmwd~~ says. *I still need my blowjob*, Barry thinks. Barry makes the same patterns with his tongue on ~~Bcxxhjmwd's~~ sex but applies a little more pressure this time. Barry is using the tip of his tongue like the eraser at the end of a no. 2 Staedler wood pencil. Barry makes sure ~~Bcxxhjmwd~~ can feel what he is doing. Barry's tongue makes deep circles. Five minutes pass. Barry tastes a little pee and becomes hard. Seven minutes pass and Barry's penis is now completely hard. Twelve minutes pass and Barry's arms begin to hurt. He stops licking and looks up at ~~Bcxxhjmwd~~. ~~Bcxxhjmwd~~ has been staring at the top of Barry's head for the whole twenty-four minutes. *I wonder what the top of my head looks like*, Barry thinks. This thought is interrupted when Barry realizes it is a little past noon. He continues what he is doing and a few moments later, ~~Bcxxhjmwd~~ moans.

We don't sleep well that night. We think about things. Like college and life. The jobs we don't have. The people we know in this life. The people we don't know in this life. How the people we know aren't actually the people we want to know anymore. How we want a new life. We take turns crying. We think, at one point, maybe, ~~mother~~ can hear, but ~~she~~ doesn't say anything, because, ~~she~~ too begins to cry—at some point—during the night.

M. Antoine invites a famous movie director to the island. It takes her thirteen days to accept the invitation and finally make her way to the island. She arrives on a giant freighter—with fish and lobster and shrimp and whale and squid—on its way to Alaska and presents seventy-three pieces of individual luggage. The movie director says, "They're mostly film canisters." She looks up at them. "But also, I wasn't sure how long I'd be staying so I planned for a long stay." Her film is a documentary on almost-instinct sea creatures and dramatic oil spills. Mostly, it turns out to be about sea turtles. And sea turtle birth cycles. The director says, during the middle of the documentary—a part where a sea turtle can be seen hatching from an egg—"This is a very rough cut and probably a bit longer than it's going to run at the festival." There is a scene involving men with beards who live on a small fishing boat in the middle of the China Sea. They go out into the middle of the ocean, several months at a time, and fish for crab and lobster. A little bit into the movie, one of them is involved in an accident and the boat hurries back to land so the man can be rushed to the hospital and all of the men with beards wait in the waiting room to hear from the doctor or the nurse about the man with the beard in the operating room and, finally, after what seems like a long time, a bald man, who the bearded men assume is the doctor, walks out and says to them, "Your friend is dead." The movie director says, "And none of the men on the ship knew Yves was diabetic. Yves—that was his name." The documentary ends a few hours later and M. Antoine compliments the woman for creating such a brave piece of modern art.

They watch another movie. Something by Woody
Allen. Davis cries three times. Simon gets up to
go to the bathroom. Tyler falls asleep several
times (he had a driver's test earlier that day, in
the morning). Todd asks Mary seventeen
questions. Thirteen about the movie, three about
the island, and one about herself. Mary takes the
group out on a midnight boat ride. Five minutes
and, "Are there sharks?" "There are no sharks,
no." "What about other fish?" Davis says. "Yes,"
Mary says to Davis and then to Cindy. "There are
other fish. Tons and tons of other fish." Kyle asks
something about the water and then together,
they peer into the water—and Mary shines a
light so they can look at the fish. They can see
some fish but not really. Shapes at first—things
that look like fish. But nothing tangible. Nothing
too real. (Fortunately, for them, they do not look
up into the sky and search for shapes).

Georges sends a telegram via messenger owl: *I have destroyed Tekhrit-Al-Ma'arh, ~~god~~ of mountain deaths. It was a success. It was grand. I have appeased the blood ~~gods~~. Next: Ra'am'hu-ul D'aahm Ti'hm.*

Dave successfully time-travels for the third time this week. Kareem, however, does not [make it].

Emanuelle says he has seen another château. "Like twenty-five miles from here, with the same people. We are not alone." "What do you mean *not alone*?" "Us. The same people—it was like looking into a mirror—I saw *us* at the other château." "The same people?" "People like us, yes, doing the same thing, living in a mansion, a château—they looked exactly like us. I don't know if it was us. But they were the same number too. Everything. Exactly the same!" "This was real?" "Yes. It was real." Davidoff is scared. "How did this happen?" "I went last week. I don't know. But also, it could be nothing." Amy yells something. "Everything, I believe, happens for a reason. Exists because it needs to exist." "When you say things like what you just said, that scares the shit out of me. And when you say that, maybe, things like what you just said could also mean nothing—or everything—that scares the shit out of me even more."

There is a bounty out, for the capture of Graam'Al-Faseeque, ~~god~~ of fortitude and existential hope. We eat from the meat of thirteen snakes and ask forgiveness. We pray for strength and guidance. We pray to Ra'am-Ap'Pataa'm for the third time that evening. Eventually, we complete the cycle and ensure our bodies are in alliance with the earth and the moon and the stars and the planets and the rest of the solar system and the galaxy and everything after that. And we set forth to capture Graam'Al-Faseeque. We take the goat. We feel cosmic vibrations. Tarik dies two times.

They spend the weekend eating sushi. Zodiac jumps onto the pool table. Georges is tired so he goes to bed early—somewhere in the east wing. Kyle naps on the duvet and Bernard decides to watch TV. It's some sort of reality television series. A Hispanic woman with blond hair flies out to Atlanta with what looks like the producers of the television show to meet a man she has never spoken to in real life. His online name is J-Reelz, and they met on Myspace and he says he is a rapper but, later, they find out his real name is actually Seephus. And he wonders, *how old is this television show and how are people still meeting on Myspace?* Seephus is an overweight African-American male in his late thirties. The Hispanic woman and Seephus do not become friends after their first encounter and she says she is angry at Seephus for tricking her into thinking he was someone he is not—a famous rapper—but Seephus doesn't see it that way and says he didn't try very hard to make it sound like a credible story and that, pretty much, it was her own fault for believing something like that. And, in the end, the producers of the show basically make the Hispanic woman and Seephus hug so it looks like a desirable conclusion to an otherwise lack-luster episode and then they do a one-month later follow-up type deal where we find out Seephus is now engaged to a woman who works as an assistant manager at a pretty big discount retail store and the Hispanic lady is still living somewhere in the ghetto and searching for something she calls, "My Prince in shining armor."

It's Friday afternoon already and the Kenzo blue
& white stripe print backpack is replaced with
two Diesel blue denim vanguarding duffle bags.

An airline disappears from out of the sky. Hiroshima happens. 248 passengers missing. Shots of famous people on a projector screen in Temecula. A montage of images and video. A baby emerges. Visual snow and crystal noise. "A museum of pink skin and dirty stuff." ~~Mother~~ cries. Arafat Mountain is born. The crater Tycho. A waterbed explodes. "This time it's for real." Spike Lee Nikes and Jheri curls. "What part of the planet do you dream the most about?" A luxury tower in the distance crumbles. The great ~~god~~ Pan and his lunar dwelling. In the prequel, Ryan Gosling learns to fly. Then, he learns to die. Lillian discovers a monster in the giant underground facility. Scientists everywhere. Everything: intentional. Life ceases to have meaning. Travis thinks, *~~god~~, why was I not born a woman*? "It's hard to believe in something when you don't really care." Rick Ross: Black batmobile / It's only new Ferrari. 1994.

During the second month, Sun Ra finally reaches his nadir and takes his own life. He leaves a letter explaining that he has gone to a distant planet, to live there forever—that he has grown tired of Earth and its people and everything else; that this new planet will become his new home in his new life. Javier discovers the body first, but doesn't tell anyone. Not at first at least. He never liked Sun Ra (or his music) and thinks *finally* and *fucking good* when he sees the body of Sun Ra.

They drink the Kool-Aid. Zodiac recites a prayer to Ra'amuul-Tamp-Iin, ~~god~~ of black, and asks forgiveness. They watch a stage production of ~~*The King in Yellow*~~ in the north corridor. Tarik plays ~~the Stranger~~.

In a short telegram message, Georges tells them he is somewhere, "South of the equator—near the Tropic of Capricorn"—looking for the body of Setesh-Apep-Sekh, ~~god~~ of desert storms and violence to foreigners.

During the middle of the night—a different kind of night—Kareem is sucked out of bed and lifted into the clear yellow-blue sky. The smell of ozone. He screams obscenities and the name of his second wife. The name of his son also. Then, his body becomes vaporized, completely, by high winds and atmospheric pressure.

At one point, we travel to several different countries and islands and peninsulas. Exotic locales like: China Island, South Korea Island, Saint Paul Island, Lonely Island, Pokoponesia Island, Rapa Iti Island, Dinosaur Island, L'île aux Enfants Island, Napuka Island, Takuu Island, Aconcagua Island, Rudolf Island, Ascension Island, Tristan da Cunha Island, Southern Thule Island, Campbell Island, Rorschach Island, Pagan Island, Eastern Hanoi Island, Babylon Island, Shell Perdidio Island, Togo Island, Cocos Island, Laurie Island, Trindade Island, Diego Garcia Island, Floreana Island, Fangataufa Island, Norfolk Island, Vison Massif Island, Snake Island, the South Keeling Islands, Dean Road Island, Puerto Escondido Island, Southern Maurismeto Islands, R'lyeh Island, Shadow Moses Island, Queen Mary II Island, Thimble Island, Anaïs Anaïs Island, New Penzance Island, McCollough Island, Robinson Crusoe Island,

Kabul Island, Shabazz Island, Pitcairn Island, Fuji Island, Macquarie Island, Samarkha Island, Pingelap Island, Pyramid Island, Harmony Island, New Ferrari Island, Easter Island, Clipperton Island, Atoll Island, Banaba Island, Isle of Genevieve, Banana Republic Island, Gorée Island, Nassir Island, Possession Island, ~~god~~ Island, Bouvet Island, Greenland Island, Graham Island, Sjaelland, Roosevelt Island, the Isle of Broken Dreams, Anticosti Island, Chiloe Island, Buru Island, K2 Island, Grinnell Island, Viti Levu Island, Sumbawa Island, St. Vincent Island & the Grenadine Islands, Hernandez Island, Quezon Island, Lopez Island, Japan Island, Taiwan Island, Bonobo Island, Black Island, Karnak Island, North Sentinel Island, Vietnam Island, Bear Island and the Philippine Islands.

The home invader falls through an unfinished part of the north corridor ceiling and for a moment—after he first sets eyes on him—Simon forgets everything and everyone.

He says, "What's going on?" "My husband,"
~~mother~~ says. "They've taken him. To Arafat
Mountain. He likes to surf. They're going to kill
him. Two men. With masks. My husband.
They're going to throw him into the face of the
volcano."

They walk with the men with masks for fifteen years. They teach them to watch the sky for letters and words and colors that have meaning. "You must do this forever."

After the panic room and shotgun blasts and
small house fires and expensive clothing and
Spike Jonze movies and Brazilian cops and
paramedics and police sirens and irreversible
blunt force trauma and loud sounds and heavy
smoke and emotional scarring and panic attacks;
they find out it was a man: the home invader,
and not a woman.

They sit in the media room and discuss even more things about the island. They look outside the window, together—out toward the observatory—at one point, because they think they can hear what maybe sounds like thunder in the distance—or the ~~monster~~—another ~~god~~ maybe. Mary tells them this is nothing to worry about—something that happens a lot on the island, "Actually." Simon says he has never been on an island or, lived on an island, ever. And Mary tells him it's very much like living anywhere else, that there should be no phobia of living on an island. But Simon says that knowing he is on an island, alone, is enough to make him feel different and scared of everything. And Tyler says he understands what Simon is talking about and Mary says she also understands but Samantha says Simon needs to, "Stop being such a fucking pussy."

At the château, periodically, they check the cameras for activity—break-ins or vandalism, that sort of thing. And one evening—on the high definition television in the basement connected to the security camera—they watch a woman shoot another woman, for no reason—on the eastern lawn. It takes them three days before they make it to the eastern lawn. After that, it takes five days to wash all the blood and offal from the grass. A month passes before they are even able to begin to forget about the smell.

"When do you come back," Kevyn says. "I'm not coming back," Mary says. "I'm never coming back." Todd says something. "It's over, I don't think—" Mary says and Simon interrupts. "You can't just do that," he says. "Leave and never look—come back. You're leaving behind friends and feelings and people and stuff." "I have stuff here—things," Mary says. "Yeah but it's not the same thing." "What is not the same thing?" Mary says. "Stuff that is from me is not the same as stuff that is from you," Simon says. "I don't need stuff that is from you," Mary says to David. Simon looks at David and says something to Todd. "Things and stuff, I don't need any of that. Everything I want and have ever needed is all right here on this island and I just don't feel like I ever need to go back to the life I lived before because that life was not a life I enjoyed living very much and every day, I felt like I was pressured into doing things I did not want to be doing and really, I never felt like I belonged anywhere and even where I was living—what I was supposed to be calling my home, it never felt like home. I was never home because I was always outside, away from my home, doing work so I could live in my home but I say living without even really meaning it. Living was not what I was doing. I was like a shell of something that was not myself, waking up every day to go do something I did not enjoy to come back *home* and do the same thing over and over and over again. But that wasn't the worst part." David looks at Todd and Simon blinks a couple times during the silence. You can hear the wetness from Simon's eyes as he blinks. "The worst part was watching the people around me, and even those I loved, doing the same thing and even feeling it worse than I did. The people who were trapped in this cycle and who had been trapped forever, knowing there really would be and was no escape for them. And knowing that I could not help them or do something to soothe their pain was the worst feeling. Since I was unable to help myself. How am I supposed to help another person if I cannot even help myself? That was my dilemma, every single day. Saying 'hello' to somebody on the street or even buying green peppers at the supermarket, I kept thinking *how can I help others if I can't even help myself*. And now, this is what I am doing, here, on this island, alone, by myself. I am trying to help myself so I can help others—those around me, people that I love, that I care about, who I am lucky to still have. I want to do something for them. And I want to do it on this island." "What are you going to do?" "I don't know that yet, how I am going to do it, or what I am going to do," Mary says. "But I am confident that with time, something will happen. It will manifest itself and it will happen. It will develop in the way it was meant to happen. And that is something I am willing to wait for to happen. I am no longer in a hurry to do anything or accomplish everything. Now, I wait for things to happen—and since I've been doing this, I've realized that things are much more interesting to me and long-lasting than before. It's a new feeling." David nods his head. "It's a good feeling, really," Mary says.

A shaman is summoned to the grounds to inspect the body of Israel. The autopsy is performed and Proust says, "Israel needs to have a good afterlife. I don't think he had a very good before-life." The shaman plays a cassette of Johnny Halliday music. He is wearing a Sibling 5 star oversized vest. They begin to wonder why they are here—their purpose at the château. The shaman does a dance. In the blue-white sky, a Goodyear Blimp flashes the words *paradise* and *lost* in squadron red lettering.

Like Robinson Crusoe, forest fires at night and
Radiohead during the day—the night sky, the
slanting blue—sometimes for long periods of
time. But mostly, names like: Cartier and Evian
and Gavin and Adam and Zach and Justin and
Yasmine and Umberto and Hector and Zomby
and Tamara.

Special Agent Dale Cooper opens his mouth to scream but no sound comes out. Cue blue strobe lights and disco lights and different types of special lights. Heavy heavy soup smoke. Doors in dark hallways too. From the fourth dimension: Pyramid Head. Angelo Badalamenti listening party. Bill Pullman guest appearance sometimes. Digital everything. Let's forget Jodorowsky's *Dune*, maybe. Oh, and also, no VHS allowed.

The words *space* and *messiah* in the satellite-
pink sky. The sound of stars and planets. The
death of a mountain.

Zodiac finds a job somewhere near Arafat Mountain. Caretaker for a castle. Zodiac is told his job is to make sure the castle is kept in a presentable state. Made to look pretty to the outside world, for when the owners finally decide to come back. Also, in case of visitors. The original owners, they left in a hurry. They waved goodbye to Zodiac and Zodiac waved back. They left with everything. Zodiac stayed on the island with the château and the workers and all the animals. The owners took the children and the dogs and the cats and the suitcases and a mountain and left on a giant speedboat. "So we can build a new castle in a new land and use the mountain—level the mountain," the husband said to Zodiac—which was supposed to be somewhere far far away. They went to Europe or South America. Antwerp maybe. Somewhere that wasn't here. Somewhere where they spoke Spanish or French. Not English.

Macintosh says, "This is the garage. The garage is where we keep the cars. We keep the cars in the garage because we don't want the cars to become old. We want the cars to be perfect, forever. We want to protect the paint on the cars because the paint is the first thing to become damaged on a car. First it begins to fade, then it rusts and after a while, it begins to chip. Here, the sun is very hot. We are closer to the equator than most other places. The garage here," and Macintosh points at an infrastructure, "is where Mr. Mahmoud stores his cars. Mr. Mahmoud owns 722 cars. 121 of them are one-of-a-kind cars. The one-of-a-kind cars, Mr. Mahmoud can never replace. You must do everything you can to protect these one-of-a-kind cars. These 121 cars are Mr. Mahmoud's life. Do you understand?" "Yes, I understand."

Macintosh is responsible for the cars in the garage. He speaks French and sometimes Créole. Macintosh is from Haiti. He is good with his hands—works really well with cars. His father was a diplomat at the embassy or something—a long time ago. And then he died. Now, Macintosh works here at the château, watching the cars in the garage. And he always talks about the one time, while he was watching a Bentley out on the west lawn, when the words *solid* and *slave* flashed across the open blue sky in bright white lettering before evaporating.

Macintosh takes Zodiac to the north garden. He walks him over to a tree. "There are five kingdoms in this world. The mineral kingdom. The plant kingdom. The animal kingdom. The human kingdom. And the angelic kingdom. You see this branch?" Zodiac sees it. "I use this branch as an anchor. This branch is from the plant kingdom. If you come to a part of this garden, and you are not sure what needs to be done, come over to this tree and look at this branch." Macintosh is a little taller than Zodiac, but the branch is wide and—for all intents and purposes—at eye level for both of them. He can't see what it is about the branch that Macintosh is showing him, but he nods. Macintosh says something else about the plant kingdom and moves on.

There is a woman who washes their clothes. She washes clothes every Tuesday. People call her Mrs. Unguentine, but nobody knows her real name. Mrs. Unguentine washes clothes because that is her job—they are told. There is no laundry room in the château, unless it is on the second level. Zodiac has no way of knowing if there is a laundry room in the château on the second level because he has never been to the second level. He is not authorized to access any part of the second level of the château. Mrs. Unguentine goes out to the river every Tuesday to wash clothes. She washes clothes by hand in the river. She never lets them follow her to the river. Mrs. Unguentine doesn't speak English either, so he is never able to thank her for washing his clothes, every Tuesday. He feels that Mrs. Unguentine, maybe, is from somewhere else. Somewhere that is far away. Somewhere that is not from here.

Fast-forward a few years. Zodiac. Alone. At home. A foreign film. From Guadalajara. The film opens with a shot of cars, yachts, private airplanes—even jet skis in one scene. The entire time, there is Arafat Mountain. At some point, there is a black hole. The black hole finds ~~god~~ and eats ~~him~~. Then it eats the mountain. The film lasts maybe 183 minutes.

She says the darkness isn't really a real darkness, more like a light-film-of-grey-with-tiny-specks-of-dust-and-flickers-of-light type darkness; like the inside of a church, after rainfall, in the middle of the forest, at night, with no roof and no ~~god~~. Zodiac contemplates and imagines and re-lives past-life experiences. Inside his head. He is terrified, and absolutely paralyzed, to realize and believe that one day—someday—he will be on his own. Not just without Mark and Theresa. But by himself, all the way. Universally. Cosmically.

"You're going to have to use your imagination if you want to make it to the other side of the island."

Dirty Beaches. ~~Father~~ kills men in the sand at night. ~~He~~ tastes scrotum and swallows rectum. ~~Father~~'s chakras are on point. ~~Father~~ discovers the ancient burial place of Mocatesh'Sayeer. ~~He~~ participates in the activity of death. ~~Father~~ is impotent. Hence, ~~father~~ is the meat stick.

Francine recites a prayer to Imhotep-D'agrhiil, ~~god~~ of space disasters—up on top of the mountain, at night—and does a sign of the cross before disappearing—forever—in a gust of smoke, wind and vapor.

It is a quiet Tuesday evening and one of the Tachyon generators fails. Marcus is forced to take the funicular into town. Rahul builds a time machine and says, "I'm going back to the year 1888. I need to fix something." The seventh day of the seventh year, something from out of the ocean—in the middle of the night—a creature, with foam and froth everywhere. The creature enters the mansion and eats a maid and drags itself back to the sea. Things begin to happen like in a scary movie. He says, "You have to shoot it in the face!" The girls sacrifice a Devon Halfnight Leflufy Selena & Justin tank on the front lawn to Y'akiir-Ma'am-Puut, ~~god~~ of asymmetrical panel fashion. A shaman tells them he has been sent back in time from Fell'Ohm-Ha'am to complete a series of *quantitative tasks*. "The locals believe something unholy is taking place on this land." Meanwhile, the Minotaur sleeps.

The home invader falls through the southern-
most ceiling of the north corridor and for a
moment—after Rénard first sets eyes on him—
they all forget why they are there.

After the panic room and shotgun blasts and goatskin pleated shorts and asbestos cakes and small house fires and broken promises and Venezuelan cops and Nicolas Cage and paramedics and police sirens and Thomas Pynchon muted horns and dramatic entrances and loud sounds and emotional scarring and irreversible blunt force trauma—they find out, all along, that it was a woman: the home invader, and not a man.

The following morning, they discover Phillipe has died in his sleep. They throw him into the sea. They say a quick prayer. Château Lafite Rothschild 1828 to celebrate. Dozens of birds fall from out of the sky. They use a catapult and Thierry calculates the angles and physics-type stuff to make it look extra spectacular.

They march: into the night, across the bridge, toward Arafat Mountain, over some hills and through the darkness—along the way, arming themselves with machetes and spears and rifles and guns and torches and plastic bags and kids with baseball bats. Joey dies of dysentery; Emma, diphtheria; Adam, typhoid fever; Jody, cholera; Mary, measles; Ted and Jonah both, smallpox; Dave, the whooping cough; Floyd, TB; scurvy takes Chris and Tim; Aaliyah, malaria.

Dave one day says, "Let's go surfing. To the other side." The men with the masks, eventually, they get to him and Dave never comes back.

A telegram message from a different château on a different island. Somewhere that is far away this time.

Darkness comes early that day. The sky tears open and the sound of trumpets and horns and wild animals. A man called Marcel at the front gates. ~~The Guardian of Light~~ is scared. Jean-Phillippe and M. _____.

Several scientists of different colors and sizes
arrive to monitor the weather patterns at Arafat
Mountain. They stay for several months and talk
about cosmic things and existential moments.
Eventually, they abandon the project and drive a
small boat out into the middle of the ocean and
drop everything—the rest of the research, the
findings, the data: everything—down into the
pits of the earth. A few days pass and they find a
box of hard drives and old pictures and
documents from a time before Arafat Mountain.
They sell the hard drives and old pictures and
documents on eBay. They meet a group of
Western European scientists on their way to the
Ural Mountains. Homer, one of the scientists—a
white man—reveals he is an alien from the
planet Y'aam-Al'Quin'Duhr who just found out
his home planet was destroyed, some two
weekends ago. Homer says, "I have good reason
to believe M. Bruce is responsible for the

destruction of my planet." Someone in the hallway coughs. Homer turns to look at the door. The door does not cough. In fact, it does nothing.

.

The Home Invasion Room, perhaps, is the most interesting of all the rooms at the château. They don't discover it until after the third week. In the Home Invasion Room, there is a man standing by himself. Behind the man, fluorescent lights laid out in the shape of letters. Some of the fluorescent lights have been on for a long time— you can tell. They flicker. And the letters lose some of their meaning. In and out. In and out. But there the man stands. He does nothing. He says nothing. He stands in front of the letters. And next door to him, the Killing Room. Full of people—always. Of all types. Nationalities and colors. Everything. And each person. On a path toward death. The ~~god~~ Ma'Cha'Chi stands in the center of the Killing Room—among all the people and the filth and the excrement and the refuse, his sex on display, for everybody to see. His skin, a dark red.

Another scenario. This time, people standing around. In a great big giant room. They are standing in a circle, these people, in a great big giant white room, inside a château. Somewhere that is far far away—somewhere that is nowhere that you know. In the mountains. A château, where there is a party. And the party is an exclusive party. This secret sort of exclusive party for wealthy people and nobles of the island. And everybody at the party knows: *this party is a secret and exclusive party for wealthy people and nobles of the island.* The wealthy people and nobles of the land, they are listening to music. And in front of the château, a sign reads: *Please do not enter, because—~~gods~~.* Down the road, quite a ways away, where it is raining, a lot, another château; with the same sign, again. *Please do not enter, because—~~gods~~.*

Something appears from out of the water—
something that looks tortured. Tired. It destroys
a coastline. Wipes out a metropolis. Obliterates
monuments. Years go by. And then; same thing.
Again. Metropolis. Coastline. Monuments. More
creatures this time, from out of the water. The
sky too. Monsters the size of asteroids. Planet
levelers. People in the mountains. A weapon is
created. A weapon that vaporizes most of the
creatures. The ocean. Planet earth along with it
too. Atomic pollution on everything. Air that
tastes like radiation. Nuclear fallout-stuff. Men
and women. Underground. The Mountain.
Doom. No idea what the sun looks like. Death
multiplied by three hundred million. And then,
seventeen billion years. A civilization from outer
space. Colonization and conquest and rape and
shit. Extreme white guilt. Disaster-piece. Single-
shot sequence. Monsters from outer space. The
size of asteroids. No more ~~gods~~. Everything gone.

"We're somewhere in the Pacific." "Off the coast of Japan." "Yes." "We're tired and we've no food." "Yes—tried contacting Japan several times already." "Japan won't answer." "No." "Yes." "It won't." "The sun is still out." "Off the coast of Japan." "I can see it." "Already." "Yes." "I know." "That was New York, with a monster in the water." "Yes." "Something is eating the people." "No." "Not from the lagoon." "Yes." "Please." "The jacket?" "No." "The sky." "Monster in the water." "Arafat Mountain." "The second dimension." "I don't know." "Imhotep-D'agrhiil." "In the sky." "Thirteen men." "Please." "Oh ~~gods~~ please, no."

Peace and universal love from 47°9 S x 126°43 W.

Arafat Mountain during the year 1492. Israeli roof knocking scare tactics. Black holes and obscure spacetime stuff. Earth magnets. A witch they call Medusa. Basquiat impersonator v.7.01.117b. Interplanetary genocides. Salaam'Am'Salaam. Incomplete sand dunes. Infinite cosmic energy. *Eyes Wide Shut V.* Somali ocean pirates and domestic violence. Dramatic oil spills. The *I Want to Believe* poster. Hôtel des Milles Collines. New York City, in the middle of a corn field. Mrs. Unguentine at the river. The words *magic* and *hour*. Intercessory prayer. Mandingo people and forever slaves. A text message from the pseudo-future about incest and psychological greed. Space rock and global warming. Lawrence of Arabia, circa 1201. The first all-black space colony. Alien technologies and instant teleportation. A new way to end people. 73 billion earth denizens. Moon Dome & Earth Planet. Yet'Yett-Armitage. ~~God~~ of the Amazon forest and cosmic horror.

At this point, Superman wishes ~~he~~ were real.

Acknowledgments

Bob Kleine / Jeanne Kleine / Jenna Adam / Katherine Kleine / Andersen Prunty / Christian Caminiti / Johnny Buse / Maia Zimmerman / Charlie Zimmerman / Austin Breed / Ken Sparling / Frank Hinton / Melissa Broder / Ken Baumann / Ofelia Hunt / Beach Sloth / Sam Pink / Noah Cicero / Cameron Pierce / Jon Garrey / Michael J. Seidlinger / J David Osborne / Tao Lin / Nick Antosca / Josh Myers / C.V. Hunt / Jordan Krall / D. Harlan Wilson / the Internet / Amber Sparks / Grant Wamack / Tosh Berman / Jesse Bradley / Louis Johnstone / Alissa Fleck / Madeleine Maccar / Beatrix Turán / Cortney Bledsoe / Barry Paul Clark / Gabino Iglesias / Nook HD+ / Kirk Jones / Dan Schwent / Abdullah Saeed / Janice Lee / Brooks Sterritt / Heidi Ruby Miller / Ben Arzate / Declan Tan / Chris Rhatigan / C. Patrick Neagle / Jamie Krueger / Sam Kang / Terry Archer-Blackburn / Tammy Nachazel / Amy Sagan / Alejandro Jodorowski / René Dumal / Terrence Malick / Nicolas Winding Refn / Adam Wingard / Kelly Reichardt / the Midwest / Grinnell College / Nate James / John Heitzman / Chris Dankland / David Markson / Ron Loewinsohn / Edouard Levé / Pierre Abidi / attemptsupon / breakbearr / monetizeyourcat / sexhaver / Nic Pizzolatto / Courtney Moore / (*Willkommen*) Julia Bingel / (*Hallo Wieder*) Karolin Bingel

In a parallel universe, Mike Kleine lives in New York and works at Penguin Books USA. In this universe, he was born in West Africa and lives somewhere in the Midwest with his partner. *Arafat Mountain* is his second book.

Other Atlatl Press Titles

Losing the Light by Brian Cartwright

Drinking Until Morning by Justin Grimbol

Hard Bodies by Justin Grimbol

Thanks For Ruining My Life by C.V. Hunt

Mastodon Farm by Mike Kleine

The Beard by Andersen Prunty

Fuckness by Andersen Prunty

Death Metal Epic (Book One: The Inverted Katabasis) by Dean Swinford

They Had Goat Heads by D. Harlan Wilson